Hold Tight, Bear!

RON MARIS

HARCOURT BRACE & COMPANY

Orlando Atlanta Austin Boston San Francisco Chicago Dallas New York
Toronto London

For some very nice people indeed

This edition is published by special arrangement with Delacorte Press,
a division of Bantam Doubleday Dell Publishing Group, Inc.

Grateful acknowledgment is made to Delacorte Press, a division of
Bantam Doubleday Dell Publishing Group, Inc. for permission to
reprint *Hold Tight, Bear!* by Ron Maris. Copyright © 1988 by
Ron Maris.

Printed in the United States of America

ISBN 0-15-300309-X

5 6 7 8 9 10   059   96 95 94

Bear and Raggety,

Little Doll and Donkey,

are going for a picnic.

Over the fields,

across the stream,

to a meadow near the woods.

Donkey is drowsy.

Raggety is tired.

"Where are you going, Bear?"

Bear walks under the tall trees,

through the cool quiet woods.

"Is anybody there?"

"Watch where you're going, Bear."

"Look out! You'll fall..."

Over and over, and BUMP!!!

"Are you hurt much, Bear?"

"I don't think so, Robin...

...but I can't climb up there."

"There they are, still fast asleep."

"Wake up, lazy Donkey!"

"Wake up, Little Doll!"

"Wake up, sleepy Raggety!"

"Follow me," says Robin.

"Through the wood," says Owl.

"How did you get down there, Bear?"

"We must pull Bear up," says Raggety.

"We can't reach down," says Owl.

"I know how!" says Little Doll.

"Wrap my sash round Donkey."

"Hang your bottom over there."

"Now reach down with your tail."

"Hold tight, Bear!" shouts everyone.

"Thank you all," says Bear.

"Home for tea," says Raggety.

"Shall I tell you again how very brave I was?" said Bear.